The New Girl . . . and Me

The New Girl...

For Wesie, and for all my real Shakeetas and Mias and D. J.s
—J. R.

For Mom and Dad
—M. P.

Atheneum Books for Young Readers · An imprint of Simon & Schuster Children's Publishing Division
1230 Avenue of the Americas · New York, New York 10020
Text copyright © 2006 by Jacqui Robbins · Illustrations copyright © 2006 by Matt Phelan · All rights reserved, including the right of reproduction in whole or in part in any form. · Book design by Polly Kanevsky and Abelardo Martínez · The text for this book is set in Calligraphic 810. · The illustrations for this book are rendered in watercolors. · Manufactured in China · First Edition · 10 9 8 7 6 5 4 3 2 1 · Library of Congress Cataloging-in-Publication Data · Robbins, Jacqui. · The new girl . . . and me/Jacqui Robbins ; illustrated by Matt Phelan.—1st ed. · p.   cm. · "A Richard Jackson Book." · Summary: Two girls become friends when Shakeeta boasts that she has an iguana named Igabelle at home, and Mia learns how to help Shakeeta "feel at home" even when she is in school. · ISBN-13: 978-0-689-86468-1 · ISBN-10: 0-689-86468-X · [1. African Americans—Fiction. 2. Friendship—Fiction. 3. Iguanas as pets—Fiction. 4. Kindergarten—Fiction. 5. Schools—Fiction.] I. Phelan, Matt, ill. II. Title · PZ7.R53265 Sh 2006 · [E]—dc22   2004009931

and Me

story by **JACQUI ROBBINS** with art by **MATT PHELAN**

A RICHARD JACKSON BOOK

Atheneum Books for Young Readers • New York London Toronto Sydney

THE FIRST DAY the new girl comes to our class,
the other girls all shout, "I'll show her around!"

When Ms. Becky asks the new girl to tell us
her name, the new girl says, "I have an iguana."
Ms. Becky says the new girl's name is Shakeeta,
and we should make her feel at home.

I ask Ms. Becky, "How can someone feel at home when she's at school?"

Ms. Becky says, "Well, Mia, that's something we say. It means to make her feel just like she does when she's at her own house."

I wonder what Shakeeta feels like
   when she is at her own house with her iguana.

   I do not think she feels that way now,
   unless her house is like school,
   and she has eighteen girls there
   who all want to show her around,

and one boy named D. J. who calls her Shakeeta Mosquita
until she says, "I'll punch you in the head!"

I think it might be fun to show Shakeeta around.
I want to know about Shakeeta and her iguana.
But I do not want to get punched in the head.

I ask Ms. Becky, "What's an iguana?"

Ms. Becky says, "Well, Mia, let's look it up."
She writes "iguana" on a card, and she gives me
a book called *100 Animals*.

I find the page that says "iguana." It has pictures of lizards.
Some of them look like dinosaurs. The words read, "Iguanas have
sharp teeth and claws. They can grow up to six feet long."

I am not sure I want to meet Shakeeta's iguana.

The second day Shakeeta comes to our class,
the other kids all decide to play soccer with D. J.

D. J. says they have an even number,
and Shakeeta can't play.

D. J. never lets me play soccer either.
I kick the ball wrong, and the other team scores.

Shakeeta tells D. J.
she isn't his friend.
D. J. tells Shakeeta
she looks like an iguana.

When D. J. says that,
the whole class laughs.
They all go to play soccer.

Shakeeta stays here with me.

I look at Shakeeta.

I think she does not feel
like she does at home,
unless at her house
she has twenty-eight boys and girls
who laugh at her, and one person
who doesn't talk to her,
even when Shakeeta's so sad
that she sniffles and wipes her eyes.

Maybe now Shakeeta would like for me to show her around.
Maybe she will punch me in the head.

I do not know what to say to Shakeeta.

"How's your iguana?" I ask.

"Fine," Shakeeta says.

She plays with her shoelace.

"I could tie your shoes two times so they won't untie," I try.

"It's called a double knot," Shakeeta says.

"I know," I say.

Shakeeta ties her shoelaces herself. She is still sniffling.
"What's an iguana, anyway?" I ask.

"It's a green lizard."

"Oh. You know, your iguana
can grow up to six feet long."

"It's still a baby."

"Oh. What's your iguana's name?"

"Igabelle."

I can't help it.
I laugh at Shakeeta's
iguana's silly name.

Now she will punch
me in the head.

Instead, she laughs too.

"You could hold her if you want,
if you come over to my house," Shakeeta says.
"You could feed her. She likes lettuce."

"I like lettuce!" I say, and Shakeeta laughs again.

IGUANA

I show Shakeeta
the *100 Animals* book.
She shows me which picture
is like her iguana.
It looks small enough to hold,
for now.

DINOSAUR

I tell Shakeeta
I thought her iguana
might look
like a dinosaur.

Shakeeta says, "Oh, Mia!"
Then she laughs.

I look at Shakeeta. I think that if, at Shakeeta's own house, she likes people who like iguanas and lettuce,

and who like to make her laugh,
then even here at school,

Shakeeta might feel right at home.